Bookworm
Buddies

Bookworm Buddies

Judy Delton

Illustrated by Alan Tiegreen

A YEARLING BOOK

Published by
Bantam Doubleday Dell Books for Young Readers
a division of
Bantam Doubleday Dell Publishing Group, Inc.
1540 Broadway
New York, New York 10036

ISBN: 0-440-40981-0

Printed in the United States of America

October 1996

10 9 8 7 6 5 4 3 2 1

CWO

For Roza and Allen Rosenberg:
Roses are red, but Roza's not blue
Cuz we three are pals, and our love's
  tried and true.

Contents

CHAPTER 1

Allergic . . . to Roger!

"**K**er*CHOO!*" sneezed Tracy Barnes. "Kerchoo, kerchoo, kerchoo!"

"Bless you," said Mrs. Peters, handing her a tissue. "Are you getting a cold, Tracy?"

Tracy shook her head. Her eyes were red, and her nose was running. "It's my allergies," she said. "In autumn there's all this pollen and stuff in the air."

The Pee Wees were at the park, raking

leaves. Raking leaves was a good deed. They raked them for neighbors who could not do yard work themselves, and they raked the park because it was part of their community. Mrs. Peters was the leader of the Pee Wees, and she believed in helping others.

Tracy leaned on her rake.

"Maybe Tracy should go sit in the bandstand," said Jody George. Jody was tieing leaf bags from his wheelchair. "There's mold in these damp leaves, and that may bother her."

"Tracy's just saying she's allergic because she doesn't want to rake," said Roger White.

"Yeah, she's allergic to working," said Sonny Stone. His mother was the assistant leader.

Rachel Myers glared at the boys. "Anyone

can see that Tracy has real allergies," she said. "You can't sneeze on purpose."

"I can," said Roger. *"Kerchoo, kerchoo, kerchoo!"*

Sonny began to sneeze too, and soon all the Pee Wees were sneezing.

"That's fake," said Rachel. "Make them stop, Mrs. Peters."

"Hey!" yelled Roger. "I'm allergic to rakes!"

"I'm allergic to parks!" shouted Sonny.

"I'm allergic to Rachel," said Roger. "And to *you*!" he said, pointing to Sonny.

"Tracy has real allergies. There's no doubt about that," said Mrs. Peters.

"They say allergies are all in your head," said Ashley Baker. Ashley was a temporary Pee Wee. She lived in California most of the time. She belonged to the Saddle Scouts there. But now she was visiting her cousins, Patty and Kenny Baker.

"They *are* in my head," sniffed Tracy. "In my nose and my eyes."

"She's had allergies since we were in kindergarten," said Mary Beth Kelly to her best friend, Molly Duff.

Molly held a big plastic trash bag open while Mary Beth raked a pile of leaves into it. "I feel sorry for Tracy," Mary Beth said. "She can't go to the fair or have any pets or pick flowers. Even if she gets out of raking, allergies are no fun."

Mrs. Peters clapped her hands and said, "I think we're through for today. We can all be proud of the good job we did. It was a lot of hard work."

As they put their rakes into the van, Mrs. Peters began to count noses. She had to be sure all the Pee Wees were there. She counted them twice. Finally she said, "I only count twelve." She frowned. "Who is missing?"

"I hope it's Roger," said Tracy with a sniff.

"So do I," said Rachel. "And I hope he stays lost."

Just as Mrs. Peters was going to organize a search party of Pee Wees, Roger popped out of a leaf bag.

"Ha!" he said. "I fooled you all!"

"Darn," said Rachel. "He almost got bagged up with the leaves."

"Roger would make good compost," joked Mary Beth.

"Well, don't play in plastic bags," said Mrs. Peters to Roger. "That's very dangerous."

"Mrs. Peters, we have thirteen Pee Wees, and thirteen is an unlucky number," said Patty Baker.

"I think we should get rid of Roger," agreed Rachel. "He'll bring us bad luck."

"We could *add* a new member, instead of

getting rid of one," said Molly. She didn't like Roger very much. He was mean and tricky. But she hated to hurt his feelings.

"Thirteen is not an unlucky number," said Mrs. Peters. "That's an old saying, and it isn't true. Thirteen is no different from any other number."

"Then why don't they have a thirteenth floor in some buildings?" asked Kevin Moe.

Mrs. Peters couldn't answer that. Teachers could answer *any* question, thought Molly. She wondered if Pee Wee leaders were not as smart as teachers.

"Let's load these bags in the van and get back to our meeting," said Mrs. Peters. "I can't wait to tell you all about the badge we're going to earn next!"

CHAPTER 2

The Boring Badge

The Pee Wees loved getting badges. All the way back to Mrs. Peters's house they talked about the new one coming up.

"I hope it isn't a raking badge," said Sonny. "My arms are tired."

"Maybe it's an allergy badge," said Lisa Ronning. "Then Tracy would get hers first."

"There's no such thing as an allergy badge, is there, Mrs. Peters?" asked Ashley. "Otherwise none of us could get it. We don't have allergies."

"It is not an allergy badge," said Mrs. Peters, laughing. "Just wait and see. You'll know soon enough what it is."

At Mrs. Peters's house the Pee Wees piled out of the van. They still had leaves sticking to their sweaters and shoes and even their hair. Mrs. Peters used a broom to brush them all off. Then they washed their hands in Mrs. Peters's bathroom and raced down the basement stairs to their meeting place.

"Tell us, tell us, tell us!" shouted Roger, banging on the table. Soon some other Pee Wees joined in his chant. They sang and pounded too.

"He has such bad manners," said Rachel. "I told Mrs. Peters we need to get a manners badge. I'd get mine in a minute, but Roger would have a lot of work to do."

Molly could not picture Roger, or even Sonny, with good manners. Both boys inter-

rupted others and talked with their mouths full of food and never said thank you or pardon me.

Mrs. Peters stood at the head of the table and waited. The Pee Wees knew what she was waiting for: quiet. She would not tell them a word about the new badge until they were quiet.

The drumming stopped. The chants got weaker. Finally it was quiet.

Mrs. Peters had a pile of books on the table in front of her. Molly tried to see what books they were, but the titles were upside down and she couldn't read them. Maybe they were books about getting their new badge!

"We all know that it's fall," said Mrs. Peters. "And the biggest thing that happens in fall, is what?"

All the Pee Wees shouted at once.

"Leaves fall!" shouted Tim Noon.

"Halloween!" shouted Kenny.

"We can't swim anymore," said Lisa.

"We could swim in fall if we were in California," said Ashley. "It's still warm there, and we can swim in our pool all the time."

"Cannot," said Tim.

"Can too!" said Ashley, getting cross.

Mrs. Peters frowned. She looked unhappy that the Pee Wees were straying from the subject.

"None of those suggestions is the biggest thing that happens in fall," she said firmly. "The biggest thing is—"

"Snow," said Patty Baker.

"Wiener roasts," said Sonny.

"School starts," said Jody. Jody was the smartest Pee Wee of all. Molly loved both Jody and Kevin, and planned on marrying one of them when she grew up. She had not decided which one yet.

"Exactly!" said Mrs. Peters eagerly. "Jody is right! School starts!"

The Pee Wees all frowned. Even though some of them liked school, they did not think it was the most important thing about fall.

"What does school have to do with a new badge?" Tracy asked Molly. "I hope it's not a school thing we have to do."

The Pee Wees all liked to keep school and scouts separate. They did not want their Pee Wee meetings to turn into lessons. They always watched to see that this did not happen. Not long ago they had had to write to pen pals, and at first that had felt too schoolish. But in the end it had turned out to be fun.

"School starts again in the fall," said Mrs. Peters. "And of course in school, the most important thing we do, is—"

"Have recess!" shouted Roger.

"Eat lunch!" said Sonny.

"Take tests," said Lisa.

"Go on field trips," said Kevin.

"No!" said their leader. She looked as if she was tired of this wordplay. "The important thing we do in school is *read*!"

A hush came over the Pee Wees. They could already read. Why did they need a badge in reading?

"It's library cards!" said Mrs. Peters triumphantly. "All the Pee Wees are going to get library cards in order to earn this badge! We'll all be bookworm buddies!"

Molly thought their leader sounded as if she was trying a little too hard to be excited. No one seemed to care about library cards. And bookworms sounded disgusting.

"Won't that be fun?" said Mrs. Peters. "All grown-ups have library cards! And it will help you in school, and introduce you to a whole new world of information."

Finally Ashley said, "I already have a library card, Mrs. Peters."

"My mom says we have a whole new world of information on our computer," said Tracy.

All the Pee Wees nodded.

"We have a whole encyclopedia on ours," said Kevin. "There's nothing in the whole world that isn't on CD-ROM."

"Computers are fine," said Mrs. Peters in a voice that sounded as if she didn't think they were fine at all. "But with books you can curl up in bed and read. Books stretch your imagination, and they don't need batteries."

The Pee Wees did not look convinced.

"I can take my laptop computer to bed," said Kenny.

Mrs. Peters acted as if she didn't hear him.

"After we all get our very own library

cards, we are going to have a reading contest," Mrs. Peters said. "There will be a wonderful prize for the one of you who reads the most books and reports on them!"

There was a low murmur among the Pee Wees. Molly could not believe her ears. Mrs. Peters was sweetening the pot with a prize! To get the Pee Wees excited about her badge project, she had to offer a reward. They had to be paid to read!

"We write book reports in school," grumbled Lisa.

"What's the prize?" asked Patty suspiciously.

"It will be a surprise," said their leader. "At our next meeting we're going to talk about library rules and the responsibility of taking care of the books we check out."

The Pee Wees groaned. *Rules* and *responsibility* were not fun Pee Wee words. They were boring school words.

Mrs. Peters tapped her pencil on her pile of books. Then she held them up and said what fun everyone would have checking out books just like this on their very own card.

The books she held up were books Molly had already read. One of them Molly wanted to read again. It was about how to camp in the woods.

As Mrs. Peters talked about books, the Pee Wees were restless. When Mrs. Stone came down the steps with a plate of chocolate cupcakes, they cheered and forgot about library cards altogether.

By the time the meeting was over and the Pee Wee song had been sung and the Pee Wee pledge recited, the only one who looked happy about the new badge was Mrs. Peters.

CHAPTER 3

No Books in
the Bathtub

"It might be fun," said Lisa on the way home. "Once I read a book about how to make jewelry boxes out of egg cartons. I gave my mom one for her birthday."

"Winning a prize might be okay," said Tim.

"I don't need a prize to get me to read," said Jody. "I like to read."

"Well, so do I," said Rachel. "But I already have a library card. And I know the rules.''

Molly loved to read. And she loved to write about the books she read. Or even talk about them. Jody was right. It was fun to read. But if she wanted that prize she'd have to begin reading right away. She knew Jody and Rachel would read lots and lots of books.

''I wonder if we can count books we've already read,'' said Mary Beth. ''I mean, then I'd have a million!''

''So would I!'' said Kenny. ''I'd have trillions!''

''I'd have zillions!'' said Roger, reaching up high to show the imaginary stack of books he had read.

''You would not,'' said Sonny. ''You didn't read a zillion books!''

The boys scuffled in the leaves. The others walked around them and left them tum-

bling on the ground, kicking and shout-ing.

The next Tuesday at their meeting, Mary Beth asked Mrs. Peters if they could count books they had read earlier.

Mrs. Peters frowned. "Well, I suppose they would count if you wrote a report on them. But I think the fun will be to read *new* books, and not just write about old ones."

Then Mrs. Peters talked about what the reports should include.

"You write your name at the top," she said, holding up a piece of paper and point-ing. "Then you write the name of the book, and the author, and then tell us what the book was about, who the main characters were, and what you liked best in the book. Keep it all on one page. One piece of pa-per."

Hands waved.

"Mrs. Peters, I can't get everything on one page," said Ashley. "I need a lot more room to tell about the plot and stuff."

"One page, Ashley. You have to learn to summarize the book in just a few sentences," said their leader.

"Ashley is getting more like Rachel all the time," whispered Mary Beth to Molly.

Ashley sighed and shook her head, as if she might not be able to do that.

"Write small," whispered Tracy. "That's what I do. Then you can get more on a page."

"Mrs. Peters, I can't fill a whole page," said Tim. "I can't write very good."

"Very well, Tim," said Mrs. Peters. "You can't write very well."

"I know it," said Tim. "That's why I can't fill a whole page."

"Just write big," whispered Molly to Tim. "That takes more room."

"Mrs. Peters," said Lisa. "The book I just read didn't have main characters."

"All stories have characters," said Mrs. Peters.

Lisa shook her head. "Mine didn't," she said. "It was about outer space. All the planets and stars and stuff."

"Oh well, that is nonfiction," said Mrs. Peters. She explained that fiction books told a made-up story and that nonfiction books told about real things.

The Pee Wees groaned. This was sounding more and more like a lot of work. It was one thing to read a book for fun, like a scary mystery, but it was another thing to write about it and to know if it was fiction or nonfiction.

While Mrs. Stone passed library books around, Mrs. Peters talked about how to find books in the library. She told them the books were arranged on the shelves alphabetically by the author's last name.

"What if we don't know the author's name?" asked Tim.

"Then you look on the library computer, or ask someone who works in the library to help you."

"The custodian?" asked Tim.

The rest of the Pee Wees giggled. They knew the custodian was not in charge of knowing author's names.

"No," said Mrs. Peters. "You ask a librarian, or a media consultant."

After that she talked about taking care of the books.

"You have to be sure and return the book by the due date," she said. "Others might be waiting for the book."

"What if I'm not through with it?" asked Tracy.

"Then you have to renew it," said their leader. "That means return it and take it out again."

"What if I lose it?" asked Sonny.

"You have to take very good care of the books, Sonny," said Mrs. Peters. "Be sure they don't get wet or dirty or misplaced. Readers must be responsible borrowers."

"Once my library book fell into the bathtub," said Lisa. "When it dried out it was all wrinkled."

"You have to be very, very careful with the books," their leader said, frowning. "And always carry them in a plastic book bag in case of rain."

"Or in case of bathtubs!" roared Roger.

After Mrs. Peters told them all the library rules and how to take books out and how to handle them, she announced, "And now I think we are ready to go and get those library cards, so that we can get started reading and reporting and earning our new badge!"

"And a prize," said Tracy. "Don't forget the prize."

CHAPTER 4

Baby Books and Dirty Looks

"If I knew what the prize was," said Tracy on the way to the library, "I'd know how hard to work at this."

"She's right," said Mary Beth to Molly. "What if it's a dumb prize like a ruler or a box of crayons? I don't want to write all those reports for that."

Molly didn't tell Mary Beth she was looking forward to writing the reports. She loved to read and write. She didn't need any prize to make her do it. But just as at school, no one liked kids who did the most work.

"All we really have to do is get our library card and *bang,* we get our badge, just like that," said Tracy.

At the library the Pee Wees filled out the forms Mrs. Nelson, the librarian, gave them. She beamed at them. "I'm so glad to have lots of new customers," she said.

"I'm already your customer," said Rachel, who didn't have to fill out the form. "I love to read."

"Me too," said Lisa. "My mom takes out books for me on her card."

All the Pee Wees nodded.

"But having your own card is different," said Mrs. Nelson.

Molly wondered why it was different. The books were the same. The due date was the same. The rules were the same. Rat's knees, it wouldn't matter if she never got a card of her own! But if Mrs. Peters and Mrs. Nelson thought it was important, it was easier to do it than to argue. And anyway, they would get a badge for it. That was reason enough.

Molly filled in her name, address, and grade. She signed her name where it said she would be responsible for the books she took out. She noticed that Tim was having trouble spelling the name of his street. He kept erasing it and starting over. Molly told him how to sound out the word. The paper was wrinkled and messy when he was through.

"Now, before you can get your actual card," said Mrs. Nelson in a businesslike voice, "one of your parents must sign the form. They have to say that they will be responsible in case you lose a book or don't return it on time."

"My mom says she has enough responsi-

bility," said Tim. "I don't think she'll sign this."

Mrs. Peters smiled. "I'll talk to her," she said.

"Now, even though you can't take the books home today," said Mrs. Nelson, "you can feel free to read them here."

Molly knew that. She came to the library all the time to read. And her mother took books home for her every week. This was turning out to be a baby badge. Mrs. Peters must be short of ideas. She was scraping the bottom of the barrel, as Molly's grandmother would say. Wasn't there a book of badges for scout leaders? Wasn't there a leader of the leaders they could call, like a 911 number for emergency assistance?

Maybe Mrs. Peters should ask the Pee Wees to come up with badge ideas. Molly could think of lots of badges she'd like to earn! A zoo badge for tending animals, an in-line skating badge, a camping-in-the-wilderness badge, a snowshoe badge, even a video games badge. Those wouldn't be baby badges.

Molly frowned. Perhaps those badges would be too dangerous. An animal might bite one of the Pee Wees. Someone could fall off their skates and hit their head on the sidewalk. A snake might attack them in the wilderness, or a bear might come into their tent and eat them.

All of a sudden Molly noticed everyone staring at her. She was the only one daydreaming. She was the only one not reading a book. It was her wild imagination at work. When it took over, she lost track of what was happening around her. Sometimes she didn't even hear people talking to her!

Molly got a book from the shelf.

"I'm taking all short books," said Sonny. "With big printing."

Roger was doing that too, Molly noticed. He had a big pile of books that looked as if they were for babies! Some of them had only three words on a page. And some pages had *no* words, just pictures! Roger had a notebook and pencil, and as soon as he opened a book, he wrote a sentence about it on a sheet of paper. In a few minutes he had ten book reports done. He took the books back to the shelf and got ten more.

"Rat's knees," whispered Molly to Mary Beth. "That's cheating!"

"Well, it's his loss," said Mary Beth, who sounded as if she was using her mother's words. "He misses out on reading good books."

Molly could not keep her attention on *The Boxcar Children.* For every page she turned, Roger had two more reports written!

Now he was reading board books.

"My baby brother has those," said Mary

Beth. "And he's only nine months old."
Now she looked alarmed too. "No one else
will have a chance," Mary Beth grumbled.

Tim asked Molly what *d-o-g* was. Then he
asked about *g-a-r-a-g-e*.

All of a sudden Lisa began to giggle at
something in her book. Rachel looked over
her shoulder, and she began to giggle too.
Before long most of the Pee Wees were gig-
gling, and Mrs. Peters had to hold up her
hand for silence.

Molly had a hard time concentrating on
her book with all the disturbances. She decided it was cozier to read in her little bed
with her lamp on after supper.

By the time Mrs. Peters said it was time to
go, Roger had almost filled his notebook,
and Molly had read only five pages. She
would not have a chance at the prize! She
gave Roger some dirty looks, but he didn't
seem to notice.

Roger was definitely the thirteenth scout. He was bad luck, no matter what Mrs. Peters said. If he left there would be twelve scouts, and the prize would be won fair and square.

Roger was definitely cheating. They probably couldn't get rid of him, but Molly could report him. If Molly reported him, would he try to get back at her? Roger liked revenge. He could be mean. But no one should get away with cheating. Especially a Pee Wee Scout!

CHAPTER **5**

Billions of Books

"**M**rs. Peters," said Rachel on the way home in the van. "Roger is reading baby books with almost no words in them. Is that fair?"

Roger stuck his tongue out at Rachel.

Mrs. Peters frowned. "I can't tell anyone what books to choose," she said thoughtfully, "but I think if any of you want to read baby books, perhaps ten of them will count as just one book report."

Rachel looked happy. "Good," she said.

Molly was glad that Roger had got caught and that she hadn't had to tattle on him. Rachel was brave. And ten baby books to one real book seemed fair.

"Those *are* real books, dummy," said Roger to Rachel when they got out of the van and started walking home.

"Hah," she replied.

When Molly got home her mother signed the library form. Her dad said, "Do you think you're ready to have a card of your own? Are you responsible?"

Molly was alarmed at her dad's words. He knew she was responsible and dependable! When she opened her mouth to tell him so, she noticed that he was smiling. He had been kidding. Mr. Duff was a great kidder.

Molly pretended to punch her dad on the arm.

"You do have to take care of the books," her dad reminded her. "When the books are on your card, if you lose one, it will be up to you to replace it."

Molly nodded. That was silly. It would never happen. How could she lose a book when she was so careful with her things?

"Nobody likes getting this badge," said Molly. "They like to read, but writing reports is too much like school. It's Roger who's bringing us bad luck. He's the thirteenth Pee Wee."

"How do you know he's the thirteenth?" asked Mr. Duff.

"Because if he left, there would be twelve," said Molly.

"If *anyone* left, there would be twelve," said Molly's mother.

Her mother was right, thought Molly. Still, twelve would be a better number than thirteen. If it was Roger who left, it would be an *extra* treat. The Pee Wees' good luck would be guaranteed. Troop 23 would be under full warranty, just like her mom's new car tires or the family washing machine.

When the phone rang it was for Molly.

"Let's take our forms back to the library tomorrow, instead of waiting for the meeting," Mary Beth said. "Then we can take piles of books out and get a head start."

"Okay," said Molly.

But when they got to the library in the morning, there was a long line of Pee Wees ahead of them. Everyone was turning in signed forms and waiting for cards.

"Rat's knees," said Molly. "Those guys will get the best books now."

"There are lots and lots of books," said Mrs. Nelson, who had overheard Molly.

But when it was finally Molly's turn and she got her card, only books about health and vitamins and tooth care were left.

"Psst!" whispered Mary Beth from behind the stacks three aisles down. "Come on over here. These are books for older kids."

Molly joined her where the books for sixth- and seventh-graders were.

"These will take longer to read," said Molly.

"But they're better books," said Mary Beth. "Some of them are even about dating. And kissing. They aren't full of simple stuff."

All of a sudden their own books seemed silly. Mary Beth was right. The books for older kids were much better.

"Maybe they won't let us take these out," said Molly.

"Pooh," said her friend. "They can't keep

us from reading what we want. We have our own cards now."

Molly took a chapter book that looked good off the shelf. It began in a church where someone's sister was getting married. It had no pictures. It was solid words.

The girls read the first sentence in lots of books, and finally they each had a pile to check out.

Molly was nervous when she took the books to the checkout desk. What if Mrs. Nelson said, "Oh, Molly, you aren't old enough to read these!" She would be embarrassed. She would have to put them all back!

But that didn't happen. Mrs. Nelson was busy showing a library helper how to arrange books on a cart. All she said when she checked out the books was, "Have a good day, Molly."

The girls ran to Mary Beth's front porch

and climbed into the big wicker chairs to read. Her mother brought them a plate of hot cookies and some lemonade.

Molly munched away and started the book about the haunted house. There were a lot of words on the first page. Big words.

"What does *e-m-p-h-a-t-i-c-a-l-l-y* mean?" Molly spelled.

Mary Beth frowned. "I'll get our dictionary," she said.

It took a long time to find the word. Finally they did.

"It's an adverb, it says. It means 'with emphasis,'" said Mary Beth.

"What is *emphasis*?" asked Molly.

Mary Beth slid her finger down the row of words.

"It says, 'prominence, stress,'" she announced.

"Rat's knees!" said Molly. "What good is a dictionary if the words that tell you what a word means are so big you can't understand them?"

"I think stress is when you worry a lot," said Mary Beth. "My mom says my dad's job is full of stress."

Molly looked at the word in her book. "It doesn't make sense," she said.

The girls closed the dictionary. Molly curled up with her new book again. Before long she came to another long word. This was not going well. It was all Roger's fault!

Molly put down her book and opened the dictionary again. This time the word wasn't there!

"What do we do when the word isn't even in the dictionary?" said Molly.

Mary Beth shrugged. "I'll ask my mom. There are three words in my book I don't know either."

Mary Beth took Molly's book and her

own and went to look for her mother. But her mother was talking to the next-door neighbor. Mary Beth asked her sister the words, but she didn't know.

"It's going to take us forever to read one book at this rate!" said Mary Beth.

"We'll never get the prize if we have to look up every word, or ask someone," said Molly.

"Let's skip the words we don't know," said Mary Beth.

What a good idea, thought Molly, and settled down again.

But skipping so many words was not working, she soon found.

"I don't know what's happening in this book!" said Molly.

"Neither do I," said Mary Beth. "Maybe we should take these books back."

The girls put their books in their book

bags and trudged back to the library. When they got there, Tim was sitting on the steps. He looked as if he was going to cry.

"Look!" he said, holding up a book with black-and-white pictures in it.

The problem was that the pictures were not all black and white. Someone had taken red, blue, and green crayons and colored some of them in.

"My baby brother did it!" said Tim. "And I don't have any money to pay for the book! Neither does my mom! Will I have to go to jail?"

Poor Tim, thought Molly. He couldn't write! He couldn't spell! And now the police were after him! It just wasn't fair.

CHAPTER 6

Jailbirds

The girls forgot all about their books with the big words. Their problem was a small one. If Tim couldn't pay for the ruined book, he might be locked up! A Pee Wee Scout in jail! At least Molly and Mary Beth couldn't be locked up for not knowing the big words.

Instead of going to the library on Tuesdays, would Troop 23 be going to visit Tim in jail? Would they be baking cookies and cakes to take to him? Maybe Mrs. Peters would have meetings in jail, instead of in her basement.

"Come with us," said Mary Beth to Tim. "Let's go to my house and think about how to save you."

The girls took their books in and returned them. Molly checked out some others that did not look very exciting but did have words that she could read. On the way back to the Kellys', she dropped them off at her house. She put the books on the hall floor and called to her mom that she was going to Mary Beth's again.

Tim was crying all the way, and tears rolled down his cheeks and onto the sidewalk. "I don't want to go to jail!" he said.

"It's your first offense," said Molly. "It might be like not wearing your seat belt. You'll just get a warning."

Mary Beth shook her head. "The book is ruined," she said. "And it's city property."

Tim cried harder.

"We'll think of something," said Molly. "Nothing is hopeless."

When they reached the Kellys', Mary Beth got erasers.

"You can't erase crayon," said Tim.

"We have to!" said Molly.

But the more they erased, the worse the book looked. The color spread to the whole page instead of just part of it. The blue mixed with the yellow and made an ugly greenish color.

"You guys are making it worse," sobbed Tim. "It looked better before."

Were they accomplices in crime, wondered Molly? Would they be jailbirds along with Tim? Earning this new badge was definitely not going well.

The three sat and looked at the book.

"Maybe," said Mary Beth, "we should cut out the bad pages and make new ones."

"Cutting pages out of a book is not a good idea," said Molly. The very thought scared her. "And we couldn't make the new ones look real. Rat's knees! What are we going to do?"

"Maybe we should just take it back and put it in the book box," said Tim.

"You'll still have to pay," said Molly sensibly. "They have your name."

At her words, Tim began to howl all over again. "My mom will kill me," he sobbed.

Molly put her arm around him. "Don't worry," she said. "I have an idea. We'll earn some money to pay for it. We'll sell something." It was the first thing she could think of to say.

"Scouts sell donuts to raise money for camp," said Tim.

"Well then, that's the answer," said Mary Beth. "We'll sell donuts."

"Where will we get them?" asked Tim.

Molly frowned. One problem led to another. Nothing was easy, it seemed.

"At the store, of course," said Mary Beth.

"We need money to buy donuts," said Molly.

"Maybe we should sell something we already have," said Mary Beth. "That would be cheaper. We've got some old Halloween stuff in our basement my mom says we should get rid of. I'll go get it."

Mary Beth came back with lots of old plastic pumpkins, goblins, and costumes.

"They look used," said Tim.

"Well, we can't be fussy," snapped Mary Beth. "We can't afford new stuff!"

They loaded the things into grocery bags and set off to sell them. When they got to the corner, Mary Beth said, "There's Tracy's house. Maybe she wants to buy some of these."

When they went to her door, Tracy answered. She didn't look glad to see them. And she didn't want to buy any costumes. She had other things on her mind.

CHAPTER 7

The Hole in the Bag

"**M**y library book is lost!" she cried. "I can't find it anyplace. I looked all over the house."

Tracy sneezed three times. Maybe she had hay fever. Or else she was crying.

"It will turn up," said Mary Beth. "It must be here someplace."

The three of them went into the house to help Tracy look.

"I'll bet someone in your family took it," said Molly. "Maybe your sister is reading it."

Tracy shook her head. "She can't read yet," she said. "And I asked my mom, and she hasn't seen it. My dad isn't even home."

Molly looked under the dining room table and under the chairs. Mary Beth looked in the kitchen and in Tracy's bedroom. Tim looked under the rugs.

"It wouldn't be under the rug. We'd see a lump," scoffed Mary Beth. "Was it a thick book?" she asked Tracy.

Tracy nodded. Then she sneezed.

"It will turn up," said Molly. "Lots of times I lose stuff and it turns up later when I'm not even looking for it. Even if you find it after it's due, you just have to pay a little fine. You don't have to buy a whole new

book. And you have two whole weeks to find it."

Tracy shook her head. "I won't," she said. "It's gone for good."

"It couldn't have walked away," said Mary Beth. "It hasn't got legs."

A book with legs struck Tim as funny. He started laughing.

"Come and help us sell this stuff," said Molly to Tracy. She told her about Tim's even worse emergency. "You'll find your book, but Tim's is ruined forever."

"I won't find it," said Tracy. She was crying now, and it wasn't allergies. "There's a hole in my book bag. I think it fell out on the way home."

"Then all we have to do is look for it on the sidewalk when we're selling this stuff," said Mary Beth. "We can do both things at once!"

Tracy didn't look very hopeful, but she

got her box of tissues and followed them down the street.

At one house a man said, "Why would I want a halloween costume? I'm too old to dress up."

"For your grandkids?" suggested Tim.

"I have none," said the man, closing the door.

At the next house a lady bought a plastic pumpkin for ten cents.

"See?" said Molly. "We've got a sale already! We've got a dime!"

"Books cost about six dollars," muttered Tim. "We'll have to sell a lot of stuff."

But by the end of the afternoon, they had sold only two more items. They had gone to twelve houses and made only forty cents. And they had not found Tracy's book along the way.

The three girls and Tim wandered back to Tracy's house and sat down on the front steps. This badge was definitely not going well.

First Roger read only baby books and would probably get the prize. Then the books Molly and Mary Beth chose had words they couldn't read. The new ones probably were boring.

Tim's book was ruined, and it looked as if it would take weeks to sell enough things to pay for it. Tracy's book was lost, and she'd have pay a fine. That is, if she found it. Molly didn't want to think what would happen if she didn't. They might have to spend their lives selling old clothes door-to-door. For something as fun as reading, this should have been the best badge of all! But it wasn't.

"It's all Roger's fault, you know," said Mary Beth. "He is the thirteenth scout. He's the one who brought us bad luck."

Everyone agreed about that. There was no

doubt that thirteen was an unlucky number. And even if it wasn't, Roger had started them all out on the wrong foot.

"Maybe we aren't old enough to take out books," said Tim. "I think I'm too young to be responsible. And I can't read anyway. Even those easy words."

"Pooh," said Tracy. "We're plenty old enough to take out books."

But Molly wondered if what Tim said was true. Tracy was a little careless to use a book bag with a hole. But maybe she hadn't known it had a hole.

And for Tim it must be awful not to be able to read! Maybe Molly could help him.

"What does that sign say, Tim?" she asked, pointing to the stop sign at the corner.

"I don't know," said Tim. He squinted. Maybe he needs glasses, thought Molly.

That would be still another problem if he did!

"*S-t-o-p*," spelled Molly. She said the sound of each letter clearly for Tim.

"Stop!" shouted Tim, as if he'd read it himself.

Tracy rolled her eyes.

Mary Beth said, "He should start with board books."

But Molly felt good. Tim had made a start. He just needed a little help.

Molly felt proud to be a help to Tim. And proud to be responsible for library books. Did her parents know what a good daughter they had? People should get credit for being good citizens!

Molly had to catch herself. Her grandma often said "Pride goes before a fall." What did that mean? Did it mean if you were proud of something you did, you tripped on a stone on the sidewalk and fell and broke your leg?

Well, that wouldn't happen to her. With all the problems she had faced in getting this badge, all the bad luck had to be behind her. How could things possibly get any worse?

When Molly got home, she found out.

CHAPTER **8**

Dog Day Afternoon

Tracy went home to try to find her book. Mary Beth went home to read. Tim just went home. To sound out words, Molly hoped.

Molly was anxious to get home to read too. She ran all the way. She threw open the front door. There were scraps of paper on the hall floor. Where were they from? Had her mother torn up the ads in the mail that said "Resident" and dropped them by mistake?

Molly bent over to pick up the scraps and saw that they looked like parts of a book. Then she looked at Skippy, who was hiding under a chair. The dog had a guilty look on his face.

Molly picked up her library books. One was fine, but the other one was only a cover! The inside was gone! On the spine Molly could see teeth marks. Skippy's teeth marks!

"Oh, *no!*" she cried. "You ate my book!" she said to Skippy. "Bad dog!"

Skippy put one paw over his face. Molly had scared him. Now she felt guilty. It wasn't really his fault. No one had told him not to eat library books.

Molly remembered that she had left them on the floor. That was careless. Careless as Tracy had been. But who could know Skippy would eat a book? He had food in his dish!

Puppies ate things sometimes, but Skippy

wasn't a puppy anymore. He wasn't exactly full-grown either. He liked to chew on bones and shoes and sticks.

Molly wondered if they did operations on dogs to remove valuable things they'd eaten. Maybe it was like in "Little Red Riding Hood," where the grandma was inside the wolf and they got her out alive and well!

Was Molly's book alive and well in Skippy's stomach?

Molly didn't think so. It would be wet and chewed. And operations on dogs were expensive. Vets were like doctors.

Molly picked up all the scraps. There were not enough to make one page, even if she glued them together. The rest of the book was in Skippy.

Molly knew she should tell her parents, but she was not ready to let them know she was not responsible. Not old enough for a library card. No, what she needed was time to think.

Now she had three books to worry about: Tim's, Tracy's, and her own. Darn that Roger! His bad luck was spreading fast.

"Is that you, Molly?" called Mrs. Duff from upstairs.

Molly hid all the book scraps in her pocket and said, "Yes, it's me."

"Was it an exciting day at the library, dear?" asked her mother, coming down the stairs. "Did you and Mary Beth get some good books?"

"Yes," said Molly. It was not a lie. They had been good books. Once. Right now one was a dead book.

"I'm going up to my room to read," said Molly. She dashed up the steps before her mother could ask to see what books she'd chosen.

In her room, Molly sat down at her desk to think. She got out a notebook and pencil to help her. It always felt better to make a list when there was a problem.

She made a big "1." Then she wrote, "Find a way to pay for Skippy's book without my parents finding out."

Actually it wasn't Skippy's book—he had no library card. But it wasn't her book either, anymore.

"2," she printed. "Help Tim earn money to pay for his book."

Last, she wrote, "3. Find Tracy's book, or help her find a way to pay for it."

Rat's knees, there seemed to be an awful lot of books missing! Molly wondered if any of the other Pee Wees were having book trouble.

When meeting day came on Tuesday, Molly found out they weren't. Everyone but Molly, Tim, and Tracy had their books safely in book bags. Not one was damaged, lost, or eaten. And lots of the Pee Wees had book reports written!

"Mrs. Peters!" said Rachel, waving her hand. "I have six book reports done!"

"I have four," said Patty Baker. "And I read a chapter out loud to my mom."

"I've got sixteen!" yelled Roger.

"But ten of your baby books make one," said Kenny. "So you really only have about one and a half."

Roger frowned and sat down.

"How many book reports have you done?" Mary Beth asked Jody.

Jody was not the kind of person to brag. That was one of the things Molly liked about him.

"Oh, not many," he said.

But Molly could see lots of books in his bag, and lots of neatly written reports sticking out of them.

"I think he's got about twenty," whispered Ashley.

"Did you tell Mrs. Peters about losing your book?" Molly asked Tracy.

Tracy shook her head. "No," she said. "We have to find it, or pay for it."

Molly noticed she said "we." Well, that was what Scouts were for. To help each other. If a Scout wouldn't help, who would?

"I'm not telling either," said Tim.

It was all right for them, thought Molly. They had already told Molly. But who would Molly tell about what Skippy had done? She felt that she had to tell someone or she'd explode. She wanted to tell her best friend, Mary Beth, but it was embarrassing to admit she had been careless. Especially after Tim and Tracy had asked Molly for help. And what could Mary Beth do? She didn't have money to pay for three books!

Molly had written three reports on favorite books she had read during the summer, but her heart wasn't in it. And she'd need a lot more than three to win the prize. Three might be enough for her badge, but what would happen when Mrs. Peters found out about the book Skippy had eaten? Would that disqualify her? Maybe what she read and wrote wouldn't count. Was there a rule that said "No badge allowed to people who were proud"? It rhymed. Or "No badge for a book read by a crook"?

Now Molly could not stop rhyming! Her mind was spinning with funny rhymes about sad subjects.

"No badge is what I hate, for a book my doggie ate."

"To the library I can jog, but my book is in my dog."

Too bad the badge wasn't for writing a poem, instead of reading a book!

Tim interrupted her thoughts by asking,

"When are you guys going to help me earn some money for the book you ruined?"

Molly frowned. "You ruined it first! Anyway, I've got problems of my own!" she said. Why wasn't Tim grateful for all her help?

Mary Beth looked at her. It wasn't like Molly to be cross with her friends. "What problems?" Mary Beth asked.

But before Molly could answer, Mrs. Peters tapped on the table. She held up a book. It was Tracy's lost book! How in the world did she get it? wondered Molly.

"Tracy, this book was turned in to the library by Mrs. Swenson, who lives in the neighborhood. She found it on the lawn. I believe it was taken out on your card."

Tracy turned bright red. But she was smiling. She might have been careless, but she had her book back! She didn't have to sell any more Halloween costumes!

Tracy thanked Mrs. Peters and put the book into her new book bag. Mrs. Peters talked about carelessness.

Rat's knees, thought Molly. One down and two to go. It was not likely that Mrs. Swenson would come up with her book or Tim's. They were probably gone forever.

CHAPTER 9

Time Is Running Out

"**W**ell, that's a relief," said Mary Beth on the way home. "Tracy was lucky."

Molly could not keep the bad news inside any longer. "Skippy ate my book!" she said. "Now I have to pay for it."

Mary Beth stopped walking. "How could he eat a book?" she asked. "Dogs don't eat paper."

"He did," said Molly. It didn't matter how or why.

"Well, we're back where we started," said Mary Beth. "I'll go home and think of what we can do."

When Molly got home she went up to her room and sat at her desk. She started to doodle in her notebook. She wrote more rhymes because it made her feel better. She wrote a poem about spring, and one about school. Then—because Skippy was on her mind—she wrote one about pets. She was so busy finding a word to rhyme with *terrier* that she forgot all about the book. It was fun to rhyme! The pet poem turned out the best, and Molly liked it. She drew a fancy frame around it with her crayon.

All week Molly read books and wrote reports. And all week she worried about how to earn money to pay the librarian.

"I have an idea!" said Mary Beth, on the phone on Monday. "Let's have a garage sale!"

"You need a lot of stuff for a garage sale," said Molly. "A garageful of stuff. Or people won't come."

"I suppose so," said Mary Beth. "All I've got is that Halloween stuff. Maybe we should look for jobs. Most people earn money from their jobs. We could look at the want ads and go to work."

"We aren't old enough," said Molly sensibly.

"We could use makeup and wear my sister's high heels," said her friend.

"We still wouldn't look like sixteen!" said Molly. "And they would probably want a note from our parents. Our mothers wouldn't lie."

"We may just have to tell Mrs. Nelson, and take out a loan or something," said Mary Beth.

Molly didn't like that idea at all. Still, time

was running out. The ruined books would be due soon at the library, and then what?

"I saw a book at the library called *101 Ways to Earn Money in Your Spare Time*," said Molly. "I'm going to check it out."

But when Molly asked Mrs. Nelson for the book, she said it was out.

"It's a very popular book," said the librarian. "All the Pee Wees have been asking for it. I'll call you when it comes in."

When it came in, Mrs. Nelson did call her, and Molly checked it out. Molly read it from cover to cover. Why did everyone want it? she wondered. All that was in it were instructions for making pots and dishes out of clay. There wasn't time for that.

Just when Molly thought earning money for the books was hopeless, the phone rang. It was Tim.

"Guess what?" he said. He didn't give

Molly time to guess. He said, "We've got this great big apple tree in our yard." He paused. Then he said, "A-p-p-l-e. Apple."

Tim could spell *apple*! It was longer than *stop*! That was good news!

"The tree has a million apples on it," he went on. "Big red ones. R-e-d. Red."

Molly sighed. This was not solving her problem.

"My mom made all these pies and stuff and gave lots of the apples to the neighbors and my aunt, but there are still zillions. My uncle picked them and put them in grocery sacks."

Molly was getting cross. This conversation was taking valuable time away from thinking about how to earn money for the lost books.

"My mom said that if we sold them, we could keep the money," Tim went on. "And

I was thinking that I'll bet we could get enough to pay for the book if we did."

"Books," corrected Molly. "My dog ate mine," she added.

Now Molly was sorry that she had been cross with Tim. Apples! What a good thing to sell! It was better than old Halloween stuff. It was legal, it was free, and they didn't have to be adults to do it!

"I'll be over in the morning!" said Molly. "Real early! That's a great idea, Tim!"

Molly hung up and called Mary Beth and Tracy, and they agreed to help.

In the morning Tim was in front of his house with the apples. Lots and lots of rosy red apples.

"My mom said we can give them away if we can't sell them," he said. "But I thought it would be better to sell them and earn our book money."

"You bet!" said Mary Beth.

Tracy had brought a sign that said FOR SALE. She set it in front of the bags of apples. "The sign is from our old car," she said. "We sold it for a hundred dollars."

"We can't get a hundred dollars for these apples," said Tim.

"We don't need a hundred dollars," said Molly. "We just need about twenty."

"Let's charge one dollar a bag," said Mary Beth.

That seemed reasonable to Molly. It was cheaper than store apples. And these were fresher.

Instead of sneezing today, Tracy was yawning. "It's my new allergy pills," she said. "I don't sneeze so much now, but the pills make me sleepy."

Molly wondered if being sleepy was better than sneezing. If Tracy fell asleep in school, she might get bad grades and fail. If one problem was solved, another one was right there to take its place, Molly thought. Tracy sat under a tree and leaned against the bags of apples. Before long she dozed off.

Tim waved his hands at the passing cars. They all slowed down. Some of the drivers smiled. Some stopped. And then a lady with pearls around her neck got out and bought four bags!

"I'm going to make applesauce," she said. "My grandson loves it."

Tim helped load the bags in her car. Molly could not believe it was this easy! People wanted apples! They paid real money for them!

When the next car stopped, a lady with three children asked if the apples made good pies.

"You bet!" said Tim. "My mom made about eight!"

The lady bought three bags and left.

"Oh, no," said Mary Beth. "Here comes trouble."

Molly looked down the street. It was a bike. Rat's knees, Roger was riding it.

CHAPTER 10

The Bad Apple

Roger skidded to a stop, dragging his shoes on the cement sidewalk. He picked up an apple and took a bite from it.

"Hey! You have to pay for that!" said Tim.

"How much?" asked Roger.

Molly tried to figure in her head. If a whole big bag of apples was one dollar, how much would just one apple cost?

"A dime," said Tracy, opening her eyes.

"Hey, look," said Roger. "There's a worm in this apple! I'm not paying for it!"

He was right. Molly could see a green worm sticking its head out of Roger's apple.

"Are there worms in all of them?" asked Mary Beth. "Our customers will be mad!"

"There were no worms in our pies," said Tim. "Roger just got a bad apple."

"Roger *is* a bad apple," muttered Mary Beth.

"Take that back!" shouted Roger.

Mary Beth wouldn't take it back. Luckily one of Tim's neighbors came outside to get in his car. Roger tossed his wormy apple down and got on his bike and sped away.

"I'm glad he got the wormy apple, instead of a real customer," said Molly. "He always brings some kind of trouble with him."

"That's because he's the thirteenth scout," said Tracy, who seemed to be wide awake now.

Soon all the apples were gone, but cus-

tomers kept coming. Tim ran into the back-
yard and got more. Finally the only apples
left were too high on the tree for the Pee
Wees to reach. Tracy took down her sign,
and they counted their money.

"Thirty-six dollars!" cried Mary Beth.
"Are you sure your mom said you could
have the money, Tim?"

Tim nodded. "We can pay for the books
right now!" he said. "Then you guys get
something for helping, and I'll give the rest
back to my mom."

Tim was smarter than Molly thought.
And generous! She could hardly believe
their book worries were almost over! Instead of the girls' having to help Tim, he
had helped them! Now it wouldn't be so
hard to confess to the lost books, because
their parents and Mrs. Nelson and Mrs. Peters would know they could pay for them.
They didn't need to borrow money or beg

for money. They had solved the problem on their own! They were responsible Pee Wees!

The four of them dashed to the library and explained about the two books to Mrs. Nelson. "And here is the money for both books!" said Molly. "The one Skippy ate, and the one Tim's baby brother colored in."

"Why, that is very responsible of you, children!" Mrs. Nelson said.

"We know," said Tim. "We did it all ourselves. And I can spell *apple* and *red*! Molly helped me."

"Good," said Mrs. Nelson. "That is wonderful news, Tim."

Mrs. Nelson did not say they were careless for leaving the books in danger. She did not say they were too young to have library cards. She said, "This is too much money, though. Those two books were getting ragged, and I was about to order new ones. I'll

only charge you five dollars for both of them."

Five dollars! If Molly had known that, she would have had to worry only half as much! And work only half as hard to pay the money back!

But Tim deserved the leftover money. It was his idea, and they were his apples.

"We'll call it even now, and we won't mention this again," said Mrs. Nelson. "Just be careful where you put your books in the future." She laughed. "We wouldn't want Skippy or the baby ruining a *new* book!"

When they left the library Molly felt as if a big weight had been lifted from her shoulders. She was free! She was not in jail! She could tell her parents! She could check more books out of the library on her card! And she could get her new badge with the rest of the Pee Wees.

As soon as Molly got home, she told her mom and dad what had happened. When she was all done, her dad said he was proud of her for taking responsibility for the book.

"I think you've learned your lesson the hard way," he said. "You'll probably take better care of your books from now on."

Parents had to say those things. They had to be sure you had learned a lesson. Well, Molly had.

At the next Pee Wee meeting, Molly told Mrs. Peters the whole story. Mrs. Peters said she was proud of Molly and Tim for what they had done, and proud of Tim for learning some new words with Molly's help. Of course, she did tack on the part about learning a lesson.

"And now we have some badges to give out!" Mrs. Peters said, "Badges to all of our bookworms!"

Molly did not want to hear about worms.

Even bookworms. She had had enough worm talk to last forever.

The new badge was beautiful! New badges always were. They were crisp and clean and had never been in the washing machine. This one had an open book on it, with make-believe words on the make-believe pages.

Badges were fun, and reading books was even more fun. Molly had to admit that Mrs. Peters had been right.

"This is my favorite badge," said Lisa.

"I'm going to go to the library every day," said Tim. "Even though I've got my badge."

"So am I," said Tracy. "I'm going to read every book in the whole place!"

"And now," Mrs. Peters went on, "we will give out our prize to the one who read the most library books and wrote the most reports."

"If Roger gets it, I'm quitting Pee Wee Scouts," said Rachel.

But he didn't. Jody did. And everyone clapped and clapped. He deserved it.

The prize was a pair of bookends shaped like spaceships. Perfect for Jody, thought Molly. Bookish but not too schoolish.

But the best prize was checking out new books on new cards. And all the Pee Wees could do that!

Ashley's hand was waving.

"Mrs. Peters, Mrs. Peters," she called. "This is my last meeting for the year! I'm going back to California for the winter. For school and the Saddle Scouts."

"That's too bad, Ashley," said their leader. "We will all miss you, but we hope to see you in spring when school's out."

"Too bad it isn't Roger who's leaving," said Rachel.

Molly nodded. She looked across the table

at Roger. He was putting something down the neck of Sonny's T-shirt. Something that looked wet and disgusting.

Well, it didn't matter. They all had their shiny new badges, Roger had not won the prize, and they all were bookworm buddies. Rat's knees, belonging to Pee Wee Scouts was fun!

Pee Wee Scout Song
(to the tune of
"Old MacDonald Had a Farm")

Scouts are helpers, Scouts have fun
Pee Wee, Pee Wee Scouts!
We sing and play when work is done,
Pee Wee, Pee Wee Scouts!

With a good deed here,
And an errand there,
Here a hand, there a hand,
Everywhere a good hand.

Scouts are helpers, Scouts have fun,
Pee Wee, Pee Wee Scouts!

⭐ Pee Wee Scout Pledge ⭐

We love our country
And our home,
Our school and neighbors too.

As Pee Wee Scouts
We pledge our best
In everything we do.